For Molly

First published 1990 by Walker Books Ltd
87 Vauxhall Walk, London SE11 5HJ

© 1990 Kady MacDonald Denton

First printed 1990
Printed and bound in Italy by L.E.G.O., Vicenza

British Library Cataloguing in Publication Data
Denton, Kady MacDonald
Janet's horses.
I. Title
823'.914[J]
ISBN 0-7445-1146-1

Janet's Horses

Kady MacDonald Denton

WALKER BOOKS
LONDON

When Mum was out, Janet liked to play horses in her room.

Angus and Anne were her two little horses.

Both horses liked to eat oats.

And to drink water.

Sometimes, Janet tucked her horses
into bed. They liked a good story.

Once upon
a time...

Sometimes, Janet dressed up the little horses.

They didn't like that game.

"We want more oats," said Anne.

"We want to play in the meadow," said Angus.

So Janet fed the horses and led them to the meadow.

The meadow felt cool and the little horses lay down.

"Up you get," said Janet. "I want to teach you new tricks."

Up you get.

The two horses could dance very well …

but jumping through a hoop was harder
and not so much fun.

"Enough!" said Angus.

"No more tricks!" said Anne.

The two horses shook their heads
and ran away.

Down the hill and into the field they ran. Soon they would be free! Soon they would be far away!

"Janet!" called Mum, as she came in.
"Anne, Angus."

"Have you had a nice time?"

"Yes," said Janet.
"My horses learned
lots of new tricks."

"Would the hungry little horses like something to eat?" asked Mum.

"Oh, yes," said Angus.

"Yes, please," said Anne.

Yes, please.

"Some oats and water?" said Mum.

"Oh, no!" said Anne.

"Not more oats!" said Angus.

"We'll have carrots and celery," said Janet. "I have two little rabbits who want to play outside!"